WHERE Would You Live?

Dear Reader

If you could choose exactly where you and your family lived, where would that be? In this book you'll find out about a wide range of interesting places where, given the same choice, many others have chosen to settle, in the past and today.

Some people make their homes near an active volcano in Sicily, Italy. They live with the constant threat of eruption from Mount Etna, and have to sweep ash from their pathways almost every day. They continue to live there because it is home.

> PEOPLE OFTEN QUOTE THE PROVERB, 'HOME IS WHERE THE HEART IS'.

Silicon Valley, in the USA, is a place where a lot of the technology in smartphones and computers was invented. Thousands of people choose to live there so they can work for some of the world's most innovative technology companies.

Many of the more unusual places to live are featured on pages 30–31. Do any of them appeal to you?

Sharon Parsons

My sincere thanks to the following people for their time, information, images and enthusiasm for this book:

The Martu, Western Australia, Australia

Doug and Rebecca Bird, Stanford University, California, the USA

AF583683

NELSON CENGAGE Learning™
For learning solutions, visit cengage.com.au

Contents

WHERE Would You Live?

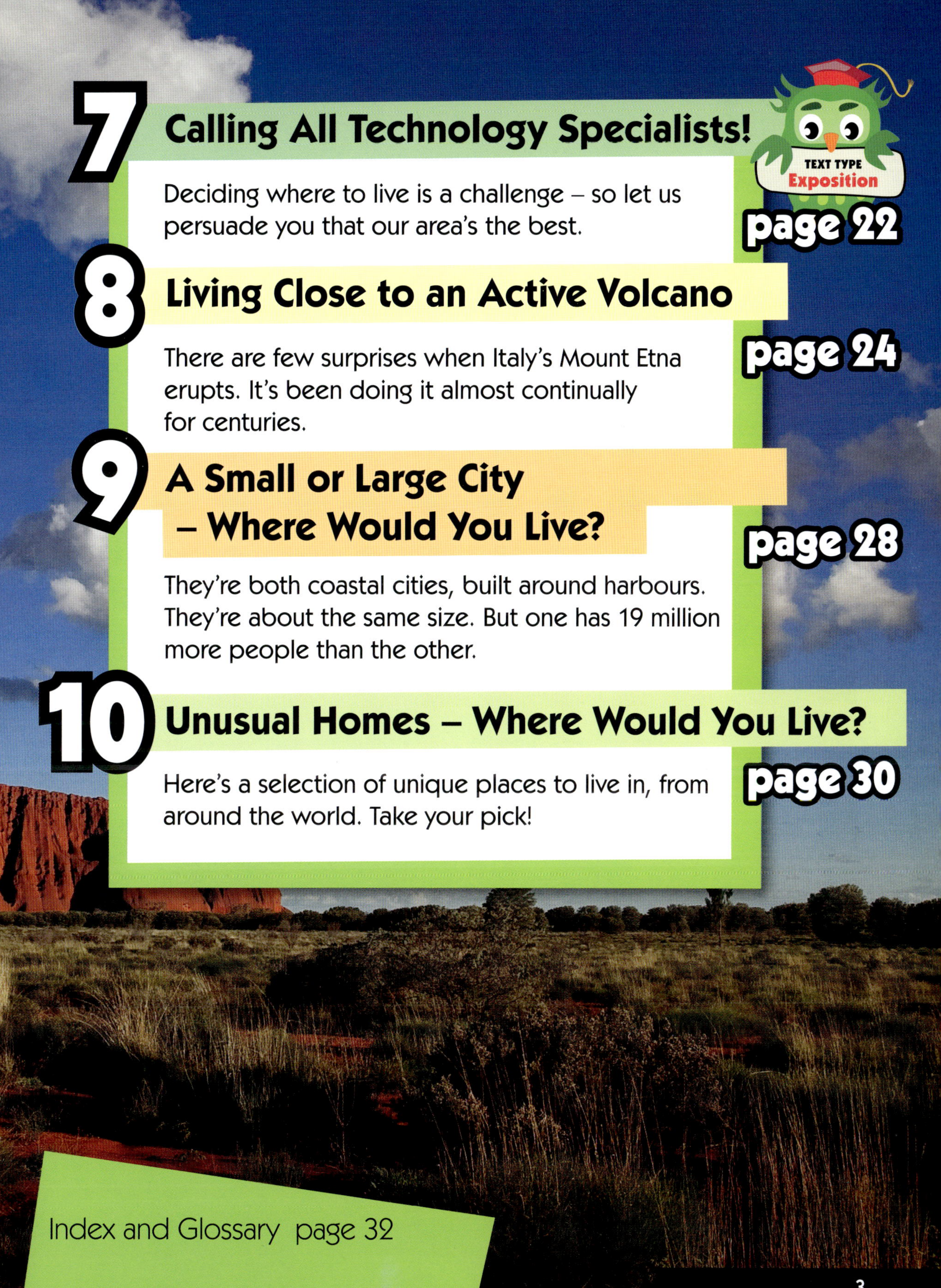

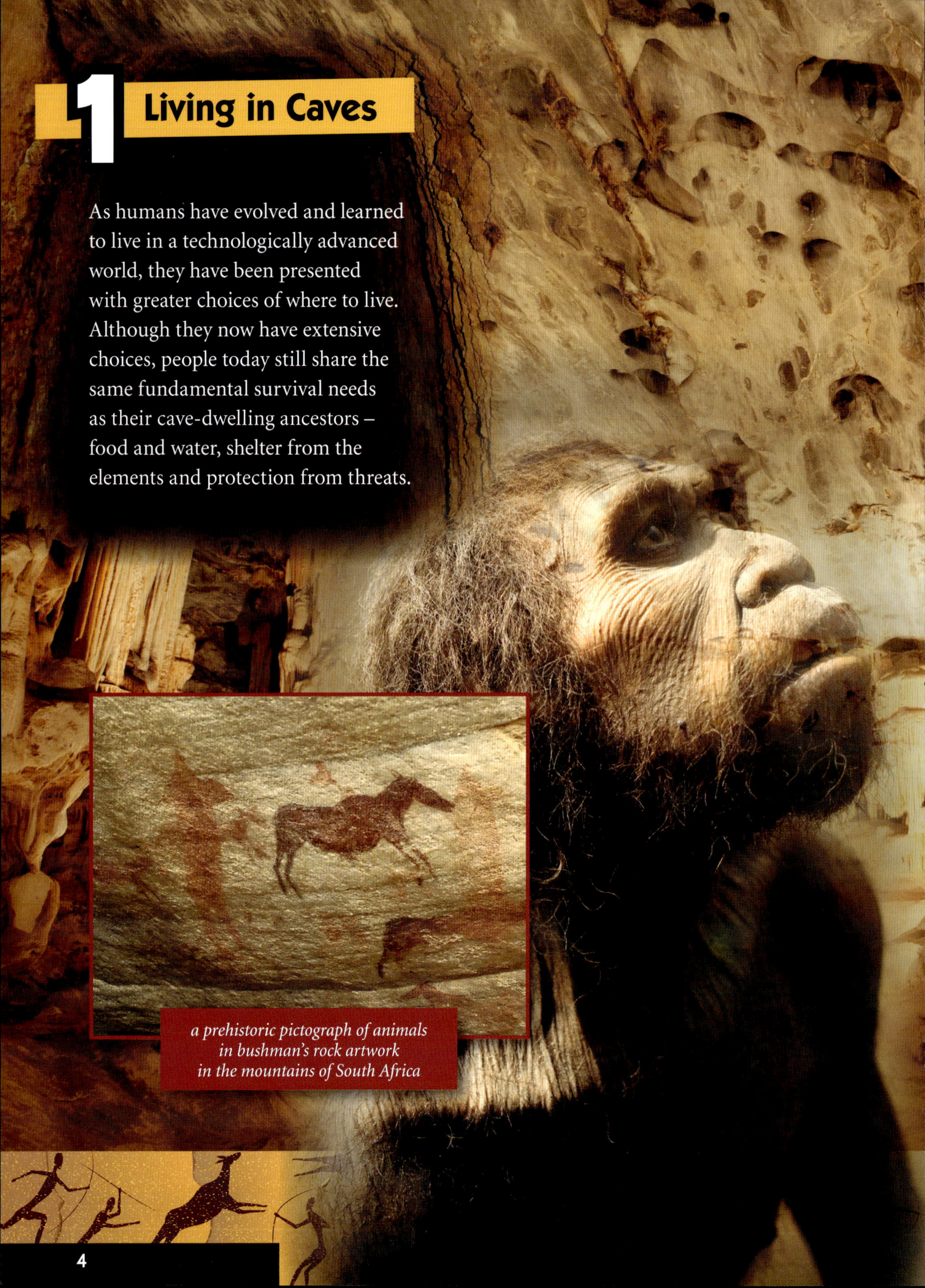

1 Living in Caves

As humans have evolved and learned to live in a technologically advanced world, they have been presented with greater choices of where to live. Although they now have extensive choices, people today still share the same fundamental survival needs as their cave-dwelling ancestors – food and water, shelter from the elements and protection from threats.

a prehistoric pictograph of animals in bushman's rock artwork in the mountains of South Africa

Earliest Life in Caves

For the earliest humans, caves provided a natural and convenient source of shelter from the weather, as well as protection from predators. Speleologists (people who study caves and their features) and archaeologists have long been aware of signs of early life in caves, such as the remains of fires, fragments of tools, animal bones and early paintings.

Discovery by Archaeologists

In 2011, archaeologists discovered what appeared to be the oldest evidence of bedding from inside a cave used around 77 000 years ago. From inside the Sibudu Cave in South Africa, investigations of the ancient beds have revealed layers of medicinal leaves, stems and grasses in sediment, measuring about three metres thick. That's quite a mattress!

ancient artwork on cave walls in the mountains of South Africa

Cango caves in Oudtshoorn, South Africa

Later Cave Dwellers in Turkey

Although humans learned to build houses from wood, reeds and other natural materials, caves continued to provide a secure and safe environment for many communities.

Early Christians and other refugees who lived in what is now the region of Cappadocia, in central Turkey, created entire underground cave cities over 3 500 years ago to keep themselves safe from persecution. The underground city of Derinkuyu was home to about 3 000 people and, because it had only a few entrances that could be blocked off, it was easily defended. Derinkuyu had five separate floors of caves, and was inhabited to a depth of about 60 metres. Caves formed in the rocky hillsides of Cappadocia provided shelter for some communities until the early part of the twentieth century.

underground caves at Derinkuyu, Cappadocia, Turkey

cave dwellings and stone houses in Goreme, Cappadocia

a view of Rose Valley from a cave entrance in Cappadocia

Living above the Škocjan Caves

Cave entrances can be visible or hidden, and vary in size and shape. The historically signicant Škocjan Caves in Slovenia have entrances underwater. In 1986, UNESCO (United Nations Educational Scientific and Cultural Organisation) inscribed the Škocjan Caves on the list of Natural and Cultural World Heritage Sites. Archaelogical researchers have uncovered evidence that people lived in the caves over 5 000 years ago. Today, the village of Škocjan is situated above the caves' site.

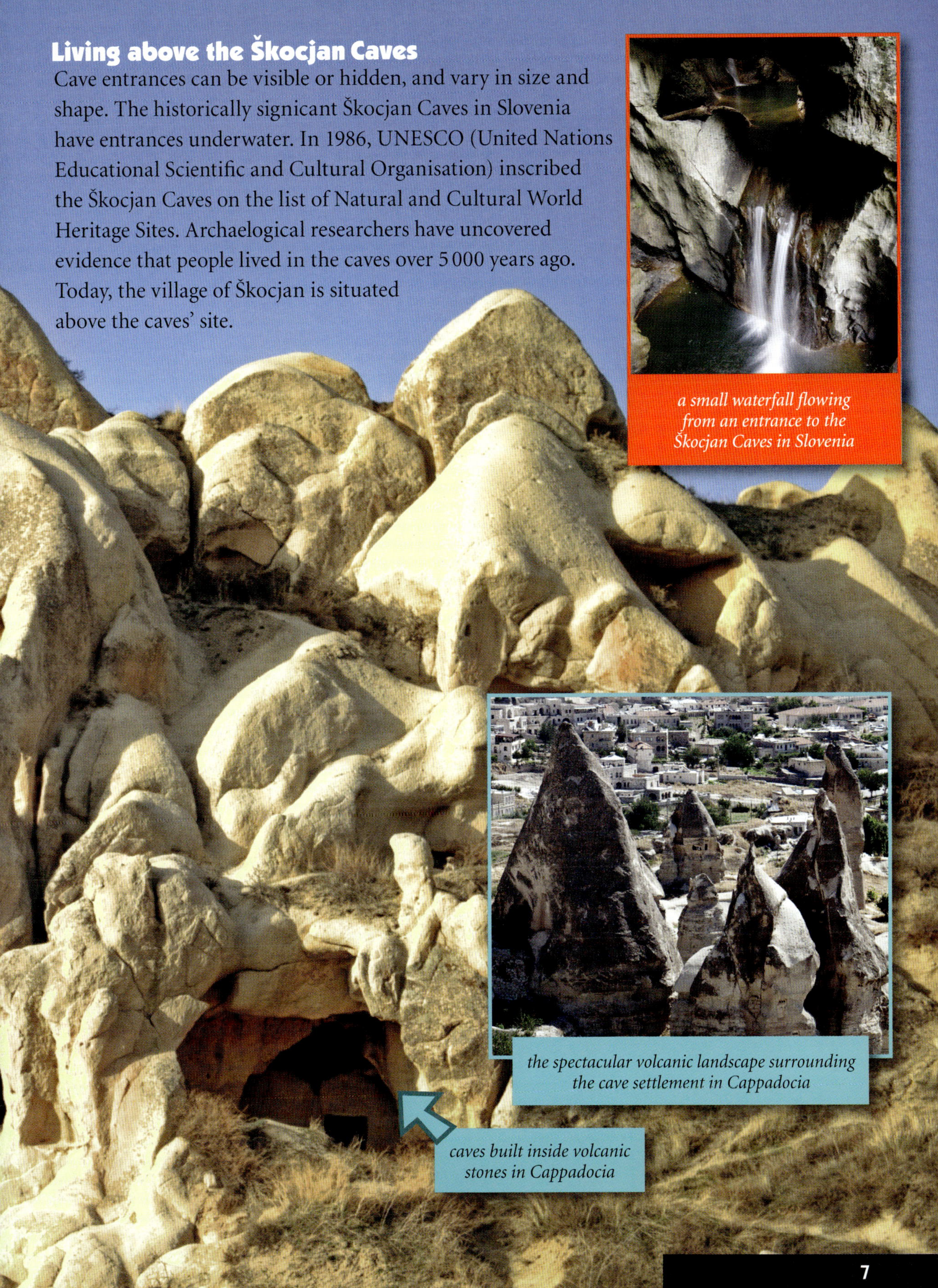

a small waterfall flowing from an entrance to the Škocjan Caves in Slovenia

the spectacular volcanic landscape surrounding the cave settlement in Cappadocia

caves built inside volcanic stones in Cappadocia

2 Cave Temples in India

Early cave temples were places of worship and for small groups of monks and communities to live in, too. The cave temples in Maharashtra, India, are famous examples of monolithic rock architecture. Indian monks and artists manually created these intricately designed and carved caves over centuries. The cave temples are a glimpse into early Indian life, and the Hindu, Buddhist and Jain religions. These Indian cave temples have been listed as a World Heritage Site.

MAHARASHTRA

Maharashtra is the richest state in India.

Ajanta Cave Temple

Intricate painted masterpieces and cave carvings at the Ajanta Caves in Maharashtra, India, date back to the first century BCE.

ancient Buddhist rock temples built into the cliff face at Ajanta

Elephanta Cave Temple

The Elephanta cave temple was constructed in the fifth century on Elephanta Island, Mumbai, Maharashtra. Among its many awe-inspiring sculptures and carvings are the giant pillars.

Ellora Cave Temples

Thirty-four cave temples at the Ellora Caves in Maharashtra were constructed over a period of about 600 years in the second century BCE.

More **Caves** in **Maharashtra**

Aurangabad Caves

The Aurangabad Caves are built on a hillside.

Kanheri Caves

The Kanheri Caves are in a national park north of Mumbai.

The Karla and Bhaja Caves

The Karla and Bhaja Caves can be reached by a steep walk that can take several minutes, but a waterfall is nearby!

a waterfall at Bhaja, Maharashtra, India

3 Nomadic Living

Instead of settling in one house or area, some people prefer to live what is known as a "nomadic lifestyle". A nomadic lifestyle means that groups or individuals move from place to place, according to their needs, seasonal variations or other factors.

When humans learned how to grow crops, many established permanent settlements around the areas they cultivated. But, for people who lived in harsh environments that would not support agriculture, such as the Bedouin people of the Sahara Desert, Africa, settling down was not an option.

The Bedouin Nomads

The Bedouin developed a lifestyle that was suited to their environment. They built portable tent structures for shelter and raised domesticated animals, such as camels, which could provide both transport and sustenance in a demanding climate.

a Bedouin camp in the Sahara Desert

a Bedouin child with the family camel before taking tourists for a ride

Advantages of Nomadic Life

In the past, an advantage of the nomadic lifestyle was that when an area became depleted of resources, such as animal feed or water, the groups living there could simply move on to somewhere else.

Another advantage was that nomads were able to trade with other groups. For example, the Bedouin people became adept at trading goods with other groups who lived on the edges of the desert, but who did not wish to travel across it.

Disadvantages of Nomadic Life

There have always been disadvantages to a nomadic lifestyle, too. Due to the transient lifestyle, it was difficult for nomadic groups to plan ahead and ensure there was an adequate food and water supply the whole year round. Temporary structures, such as tent encampments, were vulnerable to attack from other groups. Nomadic people, such as the Bedouin, needed to constantly adapt to a changing environment, whereas settled communities based on agriculture had more control over their environment, and therefore their ability to plan for the future.

With the advent of modern countries and borders, travelling from place to place has become even more difficult and many Bedouin have settled in towns and cities.

Social Studies

Modern-Day Nomads

Today, the traditional ways of nomads are being influenced by modern-day society. For example, many parents wish to provide their children with better educational opportunities, but this comes at a cost. In eastern Tibet, families are abandoning their nomadic life by selling all their animals and either moving to the city or supplementing their income with natural vegetation and crops that provide good cash income.

camels in a Bedouin camp based in the Sahara Desert, Tunisia, Africa

4 Australia's Ancient Culture

Oldest **and** Longest **Surviving Culture**

For at least 45 000 years prior to European settlement, Aboriginal and Torres Strait Islander peoples settled in many places throughout Australia. The groups led a semi-nomadic lifestyle, meaning they built permanent homes, but often travelled far to hunt and gather food.

an illustration of an Indigenous Australian dome-shaped house

Indigenous Tradition of Sustainability

Many Indigenous Australian groups have ancestral knowledge about how to live sustainably that has been passed down from generation to generation. In the past, this knowledge allowed Indigenous Australians to live in the varied and sometimes harsh landscapes of Australia. It also allowed them to preserve the diversity of flora and fauna for future generations who wish to live the same way.

Indigenous Australians and Biodiversity

A knowledge of subsistence living allowed Indigenous Australians to live off the land for thousands of years without harming the biodiversity of the Australian continent. Today, Australia is home to an impressive ten per cent of the world's biodiversity, while many developed countries have decreased biodiversity as a result of modern development.

Indigenous Aboriginal peoples used the boomerang as a weapon to hunt animals as large as kangaroos.

WHAT IS BIODIVERSITY?

Biodiversity is a term that describes the variety of species of plants, animals and microorganisms, and their genes and ecosystems, often in relation to a particular area.

Law

Convention of Biological Diversity

The Convention of Biological Diversity is an international law, signed in 1992 by 166 countries, under the guidance of the United Nations. It is designed to protect all life on Earth, conserve biodiversity and establish a sustainable, fair and equitable sharing of resources.

In Australia, laws exist to protect Indigenous rights to lands, to control access to natural resources, and to respect the cultural, economic and social impact of land development and mining of lands for non-indigenous purposes.

Burning Off Assists Biodiversity

In a Western Australian desert, about 960 kilometres north-east of Perth, the Martu Aboriginal groups still practise traditional hunting methods. This involves "burning off" patches of grass in a planned and managed way. Of particular interest to scientists is that the Martu hunting grounds have a greater biodiversity than places where burning off does not occur. On Martu lands, burning occurs in a controlled and carefully managed way. When viewed from above, the affected land can be seen as a patchwork of burnt areas and rich vegetation. Burning vegetation in this way allows a broader range of vegetation to seed and grow, therefore providing the right environment for more plants to grow. Studies show that plants and animals prefer smaller areas of vegetation, resulting from a planned approach to burning off in small areas.

A Martu hunter has knowledge of where and when to burn (and monitor) contained areas of spinifex grass to reveal the location of goanna burrows, and to reduce the number of snakes.

MARTU

The Martu is a group of about 800 Aboriginal people living on their ancestral lands in the Western Australian desert.

Traditions of Biodiversity Today

Indigenous Australians have coexisted with the natural environment and its diversity of plant and animal life for thousands of years. Their life-sustaining activities are as important in local ecosystems as the communities of flora and fauna.

Trees of Life

In the Australian desert, indigenous cultures have inherited a vast knowledge of bush foods and uses for natural vegetation. The desert bloodwood tree and the bunya pine are just two sources that have many important uses.

Desert Bloodwood Tree

The desert bloodwood tree is a source of food, drink, medicine and building materials.

Bush Coconut

The bush coconut is a combination of plant and animal, and consists of small round "galls", or parasitic lumps, which grow in the wood of the desert bloodwood tree. They are filled with water, and the outer wall tastes like coconut. On the bloodwood tree the gall is made by a female insect, which has no legs, wings or antennae, but lives and feeds on the tree and secretes a waxy coating to protect itself. The milky-white flesh of the insect larva is edible, too.

The desert bloodwood tree is a source of life-sustaining food.

"bleeding" sap on the desert bloodwood tree

The nuts on the bunya pine tree can be consumed.

The Martu desert is home to a wide variety of vegetation, such as bloodwood and witchetty bush.

Martu Hunters

Martu men and women traditionally hunt and eat smaller animals such as the sand goanna and monitor lizards. Although these animals don't yield much meat, they are easier to catch and therefore provide a reliable source of food. Occasionally, the Martu people hunt for larger prey, such as kangaroos and Australia's heaviest flying bird, the bustard.

Depending on the season, up to 50 per cent of the Martu diet still comes from the bush and wildlife – such as this monitor lizard (below) and sand goannas.

anthropologists Rebecca and Doug Bird and their children, with the Martu people

Rebecca with Karnu, one of the Martu elders

The Martu People Invite US Anthropologists to WA

In the year 2000, the Martu people were preparing to make a land claim for ownership of their ancestral lands. They invited United States anthropologists Rebecca and Doug Bird to observe and document their activity on a day-to-day basis. Rebecca and Doug had studied how Torres Strait Islanders in northern Queensland used their natural resources in everyday life, and with this knowledge they were qualified to help the Martu people with their land claim. They lived with their research team among the Martu people, documented their traditional hunting practices and prepared maps showing the locations of their sacred sites. The objective was to provide evidence of how the land and its rich biodiversity is important to the hunting and gathering subsistence culture of Martu people today. In 2002, the Western Australian government granted the Martu people native title to approximately 136 000 square kilometres of land.

5 Climate Change Refugees

On many low-lying islands and atolls in the Pacific and Indian oceans, people are finding the places that they have chosen to live are being affected by environmental changes.

In recent decades, many islands and atolls have been eroded by increasing and more intense storm surges. This series of environmental changes has reduced liveable land, affected agricultural crops, uprooted many coconut palms and infected water springs in many places. Because of rising sea levels, the people of island nations such as Tuvalu, Kiribati and the Maldives, and parts of Papua New Guinea, such as the Carteret Islands, face an uncertain future.

Some Areas Affected By Climate Change

Name	Geography	Highest Point	Population
Tuvalu 1	4 islands and 5 atolls	4.6 metres above sea level	10 500
Kiribati 2	1 island and 32 atolls	2 metres above sea level	100 000
Maldives 3	26 atolls	2.4 metres above sea level	328 000
Carteret Islands 4	5 atolls	1.5 metres above sea level	1 000

High tidal surges and rising sea levels combine to push saltwater further inland, resulting in erosion and poor conditions for growing coconut palms.

children swim in the lagoon of Funafuti atoll, Tuvalu

This aerial photograph of Funafuti atoll in Tuvalu shows how rising sea levels are eroding low-lying areas.

Climate Change Refugees

For many people affected by climate change, the question "Where would you live?" is a very real one. Faced with rising sea levels, the government of the Maldives is negotiating to buy land in India and Sri Lanka to resettle its population in the future. The government of Kiribati is talking with the government of Fiji about buying land there to house climate change refugees. Many people from Tuvalu have emigrated to New Zealand. The people of the Carteret Islands have made plans to move to nearby Bougainville.

6 Live in the Valley of Technology

Since the 1980s, Silicon Valley has been one of the world's most recognisable place names. Located in northern California, the USA, this region is home to hundreds of innovative technology companies. Silicon Valley's worldwide reputation has prompted many technology companies to base their headquarters there. Thousands of workers with information technology skills and experience live in Silicon Valley.

Origin of Silicon Valley

A journalist first used the term "Silicon Valley" in 1971, to describe the new community of electronics companies that had decided to establish their headquarters in this region – an area previously known for orchards and vineyards. One such company was Intel, which was founded in Silicon Valley in 1968, and by 1971 had invented the world's first microprocessor. The term "Silicon Valley" wasn't widely used until the 1980s, when companies in the valley (and beyond) invented personal computers, related software and hardware for home use.

History

Inventors of the Silicon Chip and the Microchip

In 1958, engineer Jack St Clair Kilby (1923–2005) invented the silicon chip while working at a company called Texas Instruments, in the USA. That single invention significantly reduced the cost of electronic functions and products. The silicon chip is a tiny integrated electronic circuit that enables electric current to flow. In 1960, Robert Noyce (1927–1990) was considered to be the co-inventor, because he designed a way for the integrated circuit to be mass-produced – this was known as the microchip. In 1968, Robert Noyce co-founded Intel, one of the largest technology companies in Silicon Valley today.

A Great Report for Silicon Valley

The global financial crisis (GFC), which began in 2007, affected economies around the world. An annual report about Silicon Valley in 2012 details evidence that the area is recovering well after the GFC, due to the performance of innovative companies such as Apple. In 2011, growth in high-performing companies created an extra 42 000 jobs.

Silicon Valley was the last region to feel the effects of the financial crisis and the first to recover. The report provides evidence that there is a good degree of job security in Silicon Valley for people who have the qualifications and proven experience. The report's findings are reinforced by an increase in the number of working-age people (25–44 years) moving to the area.

GLOBAL FINANCIAL CRISIS (GFC)

The global financial crisis (GFC) or global economic crisis (GEC) are acronyms that have been used since 2007 to describe the economic downturn in worldwide business, resulting from serious economic problems in the USA.

Billion-Dollar Battle of Two Phone Giants

Competition is fierce in Silicon Valley between mobile-phone companies aiming to be the best in the market. Each company is striving to create new and better phone features to gain market-leader status, and in doing so, there are risks that they may imitate existing technology.

In August 2011, a legal battle began between mobile phone companies Samsung and Apple. The companies were in dispute over the latest smartphone and tablet designs. Each company was claiming that the designs were originally made at their company.

a time-lapse photograph of the night sky above Silicon Valley

7 Calling All Technology Specialists!

Welcome to Silicon Valley

File Edit View Favorites Tools Help

Silicon Valley Means Innovation

Many people want to live in Silicon Valley because it's regarded as the centre of the universe for companies specialising in innovation and technology. If you're one of those people and you've got the required skills, the N-ER-G Company is looking for you!

About N-ER-G

The N-ER-G Company is a growing clean-technology business in Silicon Valley that invents all kinds of fantastic innovative green-energy products and services, such as solar panels and energy-efficient household products. Over the past ten years, we've grown from a small eight-person team to having over 1 200 employees. Our employees are technology leaders in the areas of engineering, design, science, and research and development. We've decided to expand the business by establishing a new division devoted to improving performance efficiencies of hybrid and electric vehicles.

Our Employees

Our employees describe the N-ER-G Company as a cool place to work. They say there is a positive atmosphere, fuelled by a genuine desire to create the best technologies that will help preserve the environment.

Our Offices

Our offices have been designed with energy efficiency in mind and are powered by solar-panel technology. Thanks to the increasing demand for more sustainable technologies, employment at the N-ER-G Company will ensure job security now and in the future.

a solar panel

charging the battery of an electric car

YOUNG POPULATION

About 30 per cent of the working population in Silicon Valley are aged between 25 and 44 years old.

Welcome to Silicon Valley

File Edit View Favorites Tools Help

Employee Benefits

Join our team and you will receive many employee benefits that go beyond an excellent salary and performance bonuses.

Our remuneration package includes:

- generous housing assistance to purchase or rent a property
- education allowances for children
- health insurance for the whole family
- travel allowances.

There are also numerous employee benefits and facilities to help our staff feel happy and healthy while they are at work. These include:

- sports fields for running, walking and games
- tennis, basketball and volleyball courts
- a healthcare and fitness centre, for exercise, relaxation and massage
- a cafe with free fruit and drinks
- fun games nights.

Outstanding Services

Come and live in Silicon Valley, where you will enjoy a high quality of life with all the services and facilities you need to support your family in education, health and recreation. Surrounded by mountains, valleys and beaches, with many outdoor pursuits available, a predominantly warm climate allows you to take full advantage of the picturesque Silicon Valley region and all that it has to offer. At the end of the day, come indoors to any one of the many outstanding arts and entertainment centres for music, theatre performances and museums.

An Innovative Company

Make your mark in our green-tech company! You will love living in Silicon Valley, working alongside talented people brimming with ideas and innovative solutions. What better way to help make our world a better, more sustainable place?

a downtown scene in Silicon Valley

8 Living Close to an Active Volcano

Some people make their homes under volcanic ash clouds and the continual threat of volcanic eruptions. Mount Etna in Sicily, Italy, is one of the world's most active volcanoes and holds the record for the longest period of documented eruptions, dating back to 1 500 BCE. During major eruptions Mount Etna's volcanic cone emits more lava than most other volcanoes.

"ETNA" MEANING

"Etna" is a Greek word that translates to "I burn" in English.

POPULATION STATISTICS

Sicily's population is about five million. A quarter of its residents live close to Mount Etna.

City Living at the Base of Mount Etna

Mount Etna towers above Catania, Sicily's second largest city of 300 000 people, and 18 surrounding towns, where 700 000 people live. Catania is 29 kilometres away from Mount Etna. Catania's residents are used to volcanic ash layering their city and the surrounding towns and villages. At times, the density of ash causes the airport to close. The regular ash fall causes little damage, and the locals have adapted to a daily routine of sweeping ash off doorsteps and pathways.

Living on the Slopes of the Volcano

The residents of Sicily who live on the slopes of Mount Etna say that the advantages of living there far outweigh the disadvantages. They benefit from high-producing crops and vines that thrive in the rich volcanic soil on the slopes of the mountain. Vegetation varies from the base to the top of the mountain – from citrus trees and vineyards, to chestnut and hazelnut trees, to birch trees and Etna violets near the top of the volcano.

Although Mount Etna has erupted several times in recent years, lava flows very slowly and, fortunately, no one has been killed. As a means of protection from lava flows, however, Sicilians dig tunnels and ditches around their homes. Local authorities also need to be prepared for the possibility of evacuation from nearby towns and villages in the event of a large eruption.

a view of Mount Etna and the Ionian sea from Taormina, Sicily, Italy

Mount Etna's Eruptions and Formations

Mount Etna is 3 320 metres high, and was formed from the collision of the Eurasian and African tectonic plates. Mount Etna is a stratovolcano, which means it is a volcano created from alternate layers of lava flow and exploded rock. Two types of eruptions occur at Mount Etna: explosions from its three summit craters and eruptions from its flank vents.

Eruptions from Flank Vents

Volcanic eruptions from flank vents occur less frequently but produce higher rates of lava flow.

Explosions from Summit Craters

These are regular explosions with minimal lava flow.

Mount Etna Cross-Section

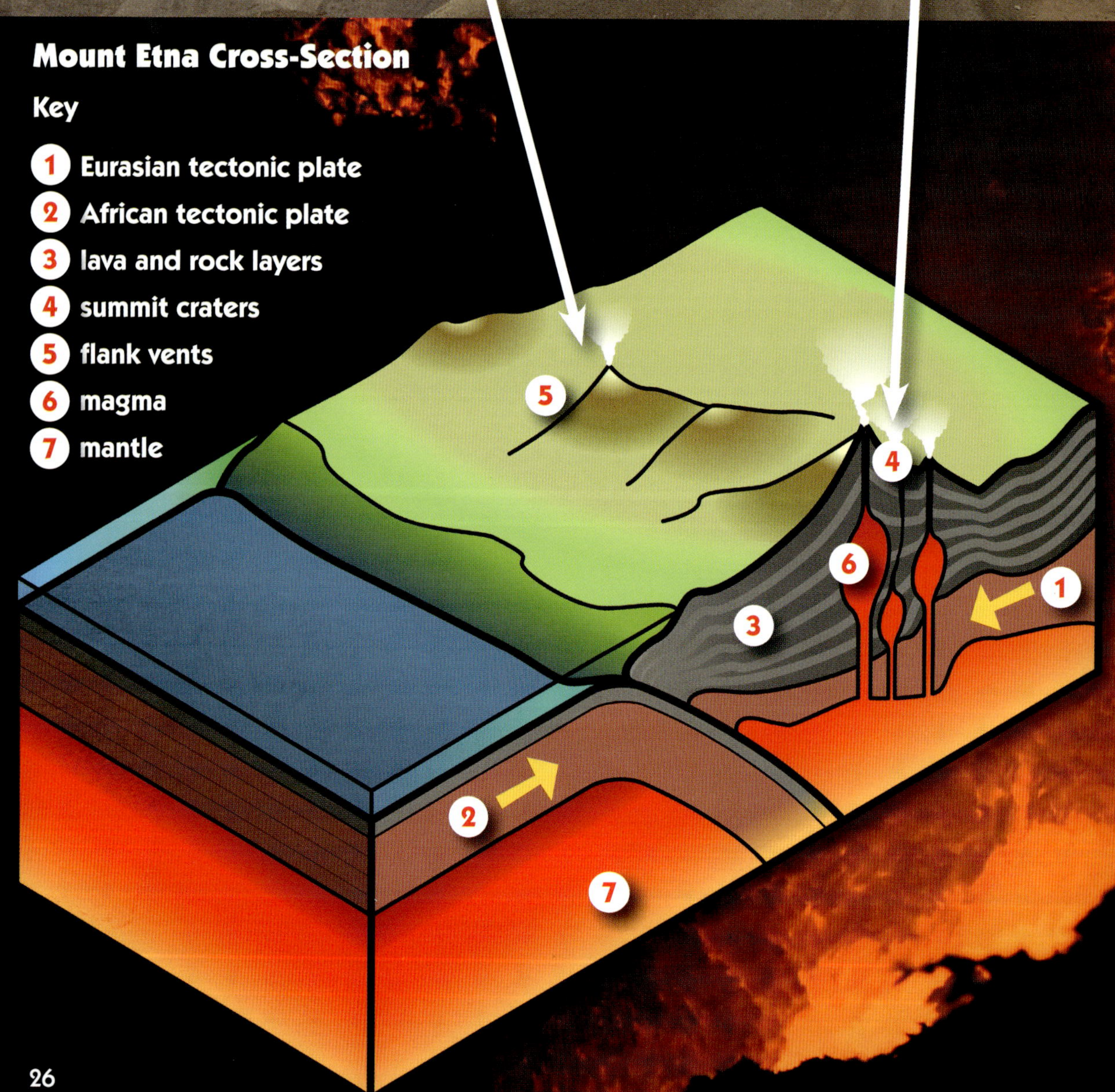

Ash-filled cloud formations are a common sight around Mount Etna.

A hot river of Mount Etna's lava slowly creeps down the mountain.

An eruption leaves a pathway of destruction and upheaval.

After the volcano stops erupting, the lava leaves a charred scar.

Tourists can view the volcanic aftermath from the crater's edge.

9 A Small or Large City – Where Would You Live?

Around twenty million people live in Mumbai, India – a city with one of the world's highest population densities. In Auckland, New Zealand, 12 300 kilometres away, only one million people live in roughly the same area as Mumbai.

POPULATION DENSITY

Population density is a statistical measure used to describe the number of people living in a given area.

Mumbai vs Auckland

	Mumbai	Auckland
City Area	484 square kilometres	531 square kilometres
Population	20 million	one million
Settlements	large numbers of high-rise apartments and slum dwellings	large numbers of single houses on parcels of land
Wealth Gap	noted for being the richest city in India but with millions of its people in slums	the largest city in New Zealand with wide socioeconomic differences between populations in different suburbs
Location	deep natural harbour	deep natural harbour
Literacy Rates	90%	99%
Film Makers	produce more films than Hollywood	relatively inactive in the filmmaking industry
Roads	congested and poorly maintained	moderately congested but well maintained
Train Systems	overcrowded and poorly maintained	reliable but limited service in some areas
Work Day Lunches	hand-delivered homemade lunches via *dabbawallas*	workers take their own lunch or buy food from cafes

skyline of Mumbai city, India

Auckland city and harbour, New Zealand

The Dabbawalla Cycle

Every day, more than four thousand *dabbawallas* (translating to "box people") deliver about 200 000 freshly made home-cooked lunches to Mumbai city office workers. The meals are carried in metal lunch containers called "tiffins". This daily tradition is fascinating for outsiders to witness, as it is a precise and punctual system – it is rare for a lunch to go undelivered. Most *dabbawallas* earn only a small fee: on average about $50 per month.

1. cycle from house to house to collect home-cooked lunches
2. cycle to a sorting place
3. transport tiffins by train to the city
4. unload tiffins from the trains
5. deliver lunches to office workers
6. collect the empty tiffins
7. return the empty tiffins to the owner's home

10 Unusual Homes – Where Would You Live?

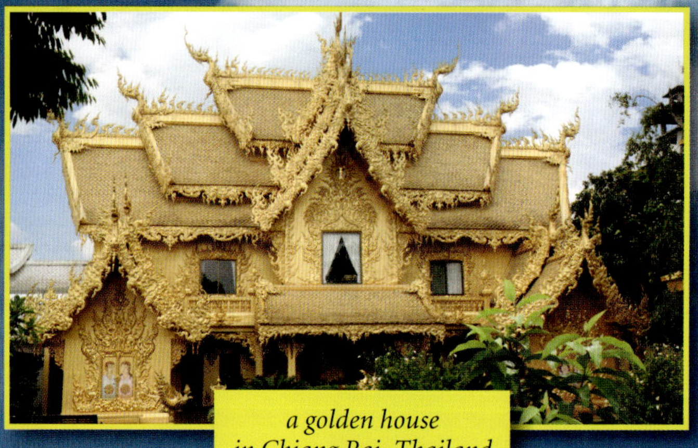

a golden house in Chiang Rai, Thailand

Caribbean houses at Panama in Central America

homes border a canal in Venice, Italy

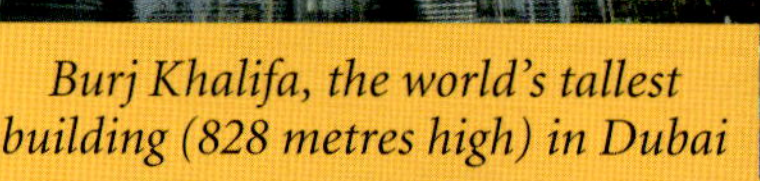

Burj Khalifa, the world's tallest building (828 metres high) in Dubai

typically colourful houses built on a hillside on Symi island, Greece

the mountain-top village of Pitigliano in Tuscany, Italy

the Hundertwasserhaus apartment complex in Vienna, Austria, famous for its colourful patchwork facade

houses line a network of waterways throughout Amsterdam, the Netherlands

a mountain cottage in Montenegro

a San Francisco firehouse converted into a home

stone and timber homes in Frankfurt, Germany

homes in the seaside village of Vernazza in Cinque Terre, Italy

the "doll lady's" house in Matlacha, Florida, USA

houses in Skógar, Iceland, with grass-covered roofs useful for insulation and filtering rainwater

homes in Beacon Hill, Boston, USA

historic homes in San Miguel de Allende, Mexico

contemporary lakeside apartments on the shore of Gooimeer in the Netherlands

modern spherical-shaped globe houses in the Netherlands

thatched Japanese gasshozukuri, or "prayer-hands", houses

Index

Glossary

archaeologists People who study cultures, especially prehistoric cultures, by excavating in the places where ancient remains are found

atoll A coral island consisting of a reef surrounding a lagoon

depleted Made less full; emptied out

hybrid The combination of two different things to produce something new, for example, a car that runs on petrol and electricity

monolithic Made of a single, huge stone or block, something that is enormous and uniform

remuneration Money paid for work or a service

subsistence living Living by using only the bare minimum of resources to survive

tectonic plates Pieces of solid rock that make up Earth's crust and upper mantle

transient Remaining in one place for only a short time before moving on